VIOLET QUESNEL

Violet Quesnel

COBY STEPHENSON

thistledown press

Thistledown Press Ltd.
118 - 20th Street West
Saskatoon, Saskatchewan, S7M 0W6
www.thistledownpress.com

Library and Archives Canada Cataloguing in Publication

Stephenson, Coby
Violet Quesnel / Coby Stephenson.

Short stories.
ISBN 978-1-927068-10-6

I. Title.

PS8637.T4828V56 2012   C813'.6   C2012-904724-4

Cover and book design by Jackie Forrie
Printed and bound in Canada

Thistledown Press gratefully acknowledges the financial assistance of the Canada Council for the Arts, the Saskatchewan Arts Board, and the Government of Canada through the Canada Book Fund for its publishing program.

ACKNOWLEDGMENTS

This book would not exist without the support of the University of Regina English Department, particularly Dr. Kathleen Wall, Dr. Michael Trussler, Dr. Susan Johnston, and Diana Lundine. Their encouragement, inspiration, wise advice, and patience is more than I could ever ask for. I also want to acknowledge the English Students' Association for supporting students' creative pursuits.

I wish to express my gratitude to Thistledown Press for taking a chance on a first-time writer and to my editor Susan Musgrave — the pleasure was all mine.

Thank you to the Saskatchewan Writers' Guild for promoting and supporting the writing craft in Saskatchewan and to Vertigo Reading Series for my first public reading as an emerging writer.

To the Original Four: Tracy Hamon, Kelly-Anne Reiss, Kat Nogue, and Natalie Thompson. Thank you for reminding me that peer pressure isn't always negative.

And never least, thank you to my parents, my sisters, and brother. Without your love, I'd still be trying to get to Hamilton.

SOURCES

Page 35. Coleridge, Samuel Taylor. "Rime of the Ancient Mariner." *The Complete Poetical Works of Samuel Taylor Coleridge.* www. gutenberg.org.

Page 48. "Down in the bootlegger cellar . . . ": Author and date unknown. This was a ditty my grandfather used to sing to me.

For Virginia

Contents

The First Time

THE CLOCK READS 6:00 AM BUT you get out of bed because of
the chirping outside your window. You didn't sleep again because
the 1984 edition of Funk & Wagnalls encyclopaedias, which your
mother earned by shopping at Safeway, distracted you. You have
read up to Volume C. You leave off at *court cupboard* and you are
already dressed for the day because you didn't undress. You glide
down the stairs trying to keep the swishing of the taffeta against
the railing to a minimum. You slip through the patio door and for a
moment the crinoline gets caught on the latch. You sit on the deck
and stare at the empty pool. The crinoline sticks to the back of
your sweaty thighs. *Formal dresses are for limousines, not lawn chairs.*
There are weeds sticking out of the pea gravel in the garden around
the pool. You know you must begin fixing this problem. Your dog,
the one that almost overdosed on your brother's Ritalin, nudges
the gravel with his nose and stays beside you. He's forgiven you
for inducing vomiting. You remember the frothing at his mouth
as he gagged up a face of sadness. He hated you. You keep pulling
those weeds as though this is your purpose, as though this is why
you were put here on Earth. The sequins begin scratching your
underarms. *Formal gowns are for dancing, not yard work.* Yes, you
have finally found your purpose and soon you grow bored and
exhausted. You sit on the deck again and light another cigarette
and think about what your father said —

"So, now what?" Your father stands in front of you blocking the
sun. Cigarette hanging from his bottom lip. "You know the rules.

You're no longer in school and you don't seem to be working; I'm sorry, but you can't live here."

He still thinks this situation is your wilful doing. After your last admission to the hospital, both your parents want to believe you are cured. They tell people you went on a vacation and took up ceramics as a hobby. Art therapy was just part of the program.

You do know the rules and then you bite the inside of your cheek because you can't let him see you cry.

⋄⋄⋄

The first time Violet Quesnel thinks about running away she is lying in bed in the damp basement. Violet can hear her sister breathing and counts four seconds between each dreaming sigh. That day at school Violet learned about Anne Frank. Lying in the dark, she thinks about Anne, and as her heart begins beating faster, the tears come. She needs to run away, but she doesn't; instead, she gets a note from the teacher the next day: "Violet didn't complete her Anne Frank assignment." The note needs a parent's signature. She gets sent to her room and sits on her bed inspecting the slug slime trails on the carpet while she cries.

The second time this feeling of flight comes Violet is in junior high school social studies watching a movie (a VHS tape with tracking problems) about the effects of industrial progress on the planet. She learns that Big Mac Styrofoam containers are causing a hole in the ozone layer the size of Disneyland. She learns that frogs are being bred with pigs. She runs to the bathroom and sobs. The world is going to end and she can't stop it so she goes home and begins scrubbing the inside of her closet with an S.O.S pad.

The third time, Violet is standing in the high school guidance counsellor's office.

She tells him: "The world is going to end."

"Have a seat, things aren't that bad," says Mr. Lowen.

Nope. Not that bad, yet. All her friends are off at university while she makes another attempt to upgrade her high school marks so she can join them. She starts thinking that if she could get enough money together, she could board a bus to Hamilton. She doesn't know anybody in Hamilton, she has no reason to go to Hamilton, but she thinks, "This would be the best plan."

Mr. Lowen asks, "Are you able to go back to class?"

Her American history teacher doesn't want her disrupting the class with outbursts about the Ford's Theatre and the Kennedy assassination.

She shrugs her shoulders as the remaining tears drip off her chin.

"Maybe your parents should come get you," he suggests.

Violet shakes her head and her hair sticks to her face.

Violet's parents are working so Mr. Lowen decides to drive her home. He is partly watching the road, partly watching Violet pinch the skin on her arms.

He tries to walk her to the door but she protests: "I'm fine. I have a key." She enters the house without looking back and then tells her sister the plan.

⊹⊹⊹

Yes, you want to go to Hamilton. You don't know anyone in Hamilton. You approach your sister while she's vacuuming because that is what she does. She is not on the road to university but is working on a work placement credit for her basic high school diploma. You shut the vacuum off with your toe and tell her the news.

"I'll help you," she says. "I'll get you on that bus."

She loves you and helps because she wants you to be happy. She conspires with you.

Janet hugs you. "Don't worry. I won't tell Mom and Dad."

You are so close to freedom. You have no money. You've been working all the time at the restaurant but have been removed from the shift schedule. You've been meaning to ask your supervisor, Joe, why, but you've focused on riding your brother's bike so you haven't had the chance. Money shouldn't be a problem though because Janet said she would help.

You declare: "Go ahead and tell everyone. I don't care."

You go to your room to pack. You grab your green carry-on Samsonite. Ugly green. Already inside:

+ 2 quarters
+ shampoo from West Virginian hotel
+ empty grape Jell-O box
+ algebra textbook
+ 3 empty prescription bottles (Lithium — 2 renewals still remaining)
+ hand towel
+ razor
+ ceramic orange bunny
+ scribbled-on loose-leaf paper with what look like hieroglyphics in the margins

You know the words made sense once. They did last night or was it the night before that? What day is today? Never mind, because you are going to Hamilton. The holes in the paper are ripped so you can't put them in a binder. Clothes. What will you wear? You start sorting through your wardrobe. You rub the taffeta from the skirt of your formal dress between your forefingers and thumbs and there is a knock at door.

"Are you ready?"

You stop. It's Janet.

"Why?" you ask.

"Hamilton. I have to get you to the bus."

Violet Quesnel

Janet doesn't love you, she just wants you gone. She wants you and everything that comes with you on the bus. It's you or her. If you go, she will be okay. If your room stayed clean, your parents would be okay. You scream but no sound comes out and you become exhausted from the screaming no one hears. If only you could lie down, but books are piled high on your unmade bed. There is another knock at the door. You don't move.

◦◦◦◦◦◦

Janet drives you towards the bus depot after she convinces you to let her in to help with the packing, but you have to make a stop first. You enter the market and begin filling your cart with fruit. Watermelon, strawberries, bananas, and nectarines will have to do. You can't touch the peaches, too fuzzy, and the grapes are seedless. Janet sees you crossing the parking lot and cries out: "Where are you going?"

You wave goodbye.

"I hate you!" she yells. You'll see her later on. You go into the restaurant where you work and start handing out fruit to the staff. You are a hero because everyone likes fruit. Then you grab your suitcase and head to the lake. Great Lake. Lake Superior. You sit on a bench and light a cigarette. You wish you could swim. The lake is a nice place to walk around, and perhaps to boat on, but the muddied waters are probably filled with pigs with webbed feet.

◦◦◦◦◦◦

Violet walks the long way home from the lake. Everyone must be in bed. She can't fit on the couch because the dog is sprawled across the cushions with his head on her favourite pillow. Violet doesn't want to sleep in her own bed. She doesn't want to get lost in her own bed. If she goes there she's afraid she'll never leave. She's

[13]

afraid she'll die alone. Also, she doesn't want to have bad dreams like when she was seven.

ᐧᐁᐧᐁᐧᐁᐧ

You dream you lose a tooth. You feel it in your mouth, on your tongue, just like a shameful secret. And then more and more teeth become loose, jagged, and monsterlike. They begin crumbling into your mouth. You can't speak. You can't swallow. You can't wake up. Your mouth is full of broken teeth. Who will stick around if when you open your mouth the only thing they'll see is a bloody smile?

ᐧᐁᐧᐁᐧᐁᐧ

Janet walks by the den and sees Violet staring at the television next to the snoring dog.

"You need to ash your cigarette." Janet gently taps Violet's hand over an ashtray. "I was worried about you after you took off. What are you watching?"

Violet tells her she doesn't want to die alone. Violet begins sobbing.

"You watch too many movies." Janet turns off the television and then takes Violet in her arms. Violet rests her head on Janet's lap as Janet strokes her hair.

Violet counts the seconds between each breath she takes. There is a buzzing that surges through her that extends from the pit of her stomach to the tips of her fingernails, from the roots of her teeth, to the split ends of each shaft of her hair.

These feelings are different from the feelings she'll have next month when she is unable to raise her arms to wash her hair.

Still awake at sunrise, she rides her brother's bike about 15 km; at least that is what the odometer reads when she gets home. She is proud of her accomplishment but she hears whispering from the kitchen after she excuses herself from the dining table, "She's getting too skinny." Violet's parents are on to her. They start to watch her eat, but she just pushes the food around on the plate. Violet is angry; she is simply not hungry, but they watch. Food makes her gag. In this scratchy nest of wrong, Violet manages to meet a young man.

⟨◦⟩⟨◦⟩⟨◦⟩

It's not your birthday, but you pretend it is. You are feeling good — great in fact. You walk into the bar like you own it. You are very beautiful and smart and everyone wants to be with you. Nothing can stop you. Not even the bouncer who will take you out the back door and leave you lying in a puddle of your own vomit as the dumpster lid squeaks in the alley wind. You stand at the bar and order a drink of sophistication — Ms. Golightly has nothing on you. You notice a pair of eye glasses out of the corner of your eye. You put your martini down and slide your arm across the bar towards the spectacles. You stop and look around to make sure no one is watching, but you want you try them on. With your new specs you look around with deadpan determination as though they are yours and notice you have an audience of one. You take them off and put them down but they want to be back, balanced on the bridge of your nose. You reach for them again and the audience cracks a smile. You slide down towards him.

"I prefer bigger frames like Elton John's — large and ridiculous."

He laughs. You take the glasses off and try to explain that they aren't even yours.

"I know," he says, "those are my friend's."

You want to be sucked into the ground, but you don't let on and continue to perform for him.

You negotiate: "I'll shave my legs for you if you call me."

You give him your phone number; well at least you think you do.

Days later you are sitting by the pool with itchy legs waiting for something or someone but you're not exactly sure what or whom. You call Pierce. He'll help.

⊖⊖⊖

There is the smell of change in the air and the days are getting shorter. People will begin to cloak themselves in bulky sweaters to hide the winter misery and indulge in second helpings of pasta with rich cream sauce. Violet thinks about a noose, but she wouldn't be able to tie the knot tight enough and even if she could, this would be an impossible task because she can't move. She can barely roll over in bed. The car warming in the garage sounds like an inviting solution but the smell of fuel makes her nauseated.

These days it hurts for her to try. To try what? Just to *try*. It feels like she has swallowed a stone. Perhaps this heavy feeling will make it easier to sink to the bottom of Lake Superior. Even the fine hairs on her chin feel heavy. She worries that one day she'll slow down so much that even blinking will cease.

How is she feeling?

"Thick as a bowl of gumbo."

Pierce isn't coming to help Violet. Her mouth is so dry and her tongue is heavy. She can no longer pick out Hamilton on a map. Violet just sleeps.

Violet hears knocking. It's Janet.

"Remember the plan?"

Violet doesn't answer. Janet opens the door anyway and can't see her sister behind the stack of encyclopedias.

"Leave me alone," Violet says.

"I thought maybe we should try getting you on that bus to Hamilton. It's getting colder out and so you'll have to find a place to live. Let me help you pack."

Janet grabs the green suitcase. She removes the items Violet previously collected.

"You don't need this stuff." She throws the papers and the Jell-O box into the wastebasket and opens the dresser drawer and grabs a handful of socks.

"Didn't I pack well enough the first time?"

"You did fine, just fine. Don't you want some comfy clothes to wear?"

Later, Janet helps Violet wash her hair. She even puts toothpaste on Violet's toothbrush and moves Violet's hand up and down. As the frothing paste drips down her chin, Violet says, "I'll miss you."

⊹⊹⊹

In the end, it didn't matter how or what you packed, or the fact that you couldn't execute simple hygienic tasks let alone be able to navigate a city you'd never been to before, because you never made it to Hamilton. Instead, unbeknownst to you, your father overheard you and Janet whispering about the plan you two made together. He approached Janet and demanded that she continue to play along but instead of taking you to the bus depot, someone would be waiting to greet you at the Emergency entrance.

The News

SHE DIDN'T RUN AWAY BECAUSE SHE wasn't that brave. Her father, Stanley, rescued her. They drove in silence west along the highway with her few belongings in the back of his green truck. She was grateful to see the horizon again because the winding and jerking of the truck through the Shield had intensified her nausea. Violet's father never questioned why she needed him to pull over to the side of the road so she could vomit in the ditch along the Trans-Canada. He probably just assumed she was detoxifying *en route* as he was aware that she got into trouble with self-medicating from time to time. Her nausea was mixed with guilt, for Violet had a secret that would change his life forever, too.

Earlier that year, Stanley Quesnel moved his family to Regina because he wanted to be closer to his mother who was suffering from dementia. Violet refused to move with them, and so had remained in the Soo where her psychiatric support team would be there to catch her when she fell.

"Would you like a cigarette?" he asked, while rolling down his window and pushing in the lighter.

Violet shook her head as she reached into her pocket and tossed a half-pack of *Benson & Hedges 100s* onto the dash. "Here, you can have these."

On the second day after leaving Sault Ste. Marie with Stanley smoking and Violet vomiting, they arrived in Regina. No one greeted them at the door. The family didn't say much because they knew, all too well, that you shouldn't antagonize the mentally ill. Well, everyone except her youngest sister, Beth.

"So, Violet gets depressed and Dad as usual has to drop everything to save her sorry ass from the loony bin." Beth was never at a loss for words. "When are you going to get it together, Violet?"

Holding her green suitcase with white knuckles, Violet paused to watch her sister lick mayonnaise off a butter knife.

"What makes you so special that time has to stand still for everyone in the family just because you were having a rough day and had one too many? It's getting old." Beth never really understood.

Violet continued to stare as Beth juggled luncheon meat, processed cheese slices, and a jar of pickles while trying to open the refrigerator.

"Hold your breath everyone, Violet can't remember who dragged her sorry ass down to Emergency and dumped her into a wheelchair in the parking lot — again."

It was easy for Beth to lay the cards of someone else's hand on the table. It distracted her from thinking about her own life and the shithead she got her legs tangled with.

"I've missed you, too," said Violet. "So, where's Mr. Wonderful?"

Beth huffed as she inhaled her sandwich and walked towards the den.

Violet continued through the kitchen and went upstairs to unpack. She had gone over it a million times in her head. It was going to be difficult to gather enough courage to reveal to her mother that she was pregnant. Every day, for two weeks, Violet tiptoed around the house being careful not to cause trouble and then the opportunity came while her mother Judy was making dinner. She reacted just as Violet had predicted.

"You are not going to be able to take care of a child! You are not well. You can hardly take care of yourself."

The knife slipped and cut into her mother's finger.

"Christ, see what you made me do?" Judy grabbed a paper towel and began wrapping it around the wound.

Judy had difficulty addressing bipolar disorder in a mature, frank manner. Saying *not well* was like chewing steel wool for Violet. She ran to her room weeping, not because her mother's comments hurt, and not because of the blood-soaked paper towel, but because she was courageous enough to tell her mother and now her pregnancy was no longer a secret. She slammed the door and looked at her face in the mirror.

⌀⌀⌀

It was the fall of 1997, she was fabulously underweight, always drunk, and void of a reason to live. The leaves were brilliant hues of reds and oranges, but Violet didn't care to notice. One numb night she attended a staff party. As a rule she hated parties but the festivities made her drunken state look social. Unfortunately, Jason showed up with his latest edition. She couldn't handle envy and humiliation. Her breath was shallow. She reacted just as people predicted when Jason arrived. Violet was escorted from the party in complete disrepair, but not without saying goodbye to Jason and his new girlfriend.

"You have the nerve to bring your latest conquest knowing I would be here! Rot in hell!" Violet turned her attention to Jason's date, "You'll have about two good months and then he'll find a fresh one!"

Violet was dropped off at what had become her second home on the second floor at Avondale Memorial. Yes, being a guest at the hospital was nothing new to her. The charge nurse checked her into her room: "We'll talk about what happened in the morning. The doctor should be in around 9:00 AM."

What Violet thought she heard was: "Ah, Ms. Quesnel. It's so nice to see you again. We'll have your private suite ready shortly.

[20]

We weren't expecting you so soon. Who broke your heart this time?"

The hospital had been a safe place for Violet since she had her first struggle with depression at the age of eighteen, but this was always a temporary fix because old habits die hard.

The next morning, after an agitated night of fighting the onset of reality, she felt peculiar. It wasn't the usual hangover that consisted of a headache, dry mouth, and Violet moaning the empty promise to never drink rye again. This feeling of unease went deeper than anything she had experienced before. A doctor she had never met had ordered blood work to check levels, whatever that meant.

"You're pregnant and as result you will not receive any more medication," he said the next day when he made his rounds. Violet stared through the doctor. She didn't know what was more shocking, the news that she was carrying another life or that her pain would not be eased with pills. He left the room as quickly as he had delivered the good news. At least this is how she remembers it. She didn't know if this was actually happening or if it was a hallucinatory effect of withdrawal. This confusion was short lived because her regular physician, Dr. Claude, visited her later on that morning. She told Violet about a couple she knew.

"Violet, they are very good people. They have been trying to have a baby on their own but are now looking to adopt. They are both doctors."

Violet looked away from Dr. Claude as her eyes glossed with tears.

"Well, you think about it." Then with a wave of a pen over a form on her clipboard, Dr. Claude left the room. She never met with the doctor couple and she never saw Dr. Claude again.

She sat on her bed pinching the fleshy part between her thumb and her index finger.

She made her way to the patient pay phone and called Jason.

The quarter slid through the slot. What brought them together was the very thing that should have kept them apart. Their need to fill a void, their need to be compulsive, their need to have the last word.

"Is the baby mine?"

"I'm not even sure if the baby is mine," she snapped back.

She hung up, hoping he would continue on with his life according to his plans, hoping that the telephone conversation would be the last time she would have to talk to him. But he surprised her at the hospital. After clearing security he met with Violet in the patients' common area. They sat across from each other surrounded by schizophrenics, bulimics, and addicts. She could tell he was very uncomfortable and this gave her immense pleasure.

"You look really good," said Jason. He always knew the right things to say to her. "I've talked it over with my mom and she agrees that having this child is not a good idea. We'll take you to the clinic."

"Of course you told your mother. I'm meant to have this baby whether you like it or not."

"You shouldn't have a baby to feel loved," he said.

These words will haunt her until the day she dies.

That was the last she heard from Jason.

❦

When Stanley came home from work that night he was greeted by his wife and the news that he was going to be a grandfather. He slowly walked up the stairs and froze outside the spare room for a moment. Violet didn't move. He sighed and continued down the hall. He changed out of his suit and called for Violet.

When she entered her parents' bedroom her father was seated on the edge of the bed; the very bed where his children were planned and created with love. He pulled her to his lap and he began to sob. She had seen her father cry only once before and that was at his father's funeral. His face was twisted and strained as tears slowly dripped down his stubbled cheek. Even stone can melt. She did not cry with him.

The Stain

THE FIRST TIME SHE GOT HER period she wanted God to take
it back. The blood wasn't rich ruby, sparkling like Dorothy's
shoes — it was filthy. She could never get the stain out. She should
have wrapped the underwear, white cotton briefs crusted with dull
rusty brown, in toilet paper and then thrown the filthy wad in the
garbage.

But what if the neighbour's dog gets out in the middle of the night?
What if he sniffs at the garbage on the curb and then claws a hole in
the bag? What if he finds the panties and then drags my filth out onto
the lawn. What if the panties lie there to be discovered first thing in the
morning by my father's car pool?

She threw them in a pile of clothes beside her bed.

❧❧❧

Calgary. November, 1986: Violet's biology class went to the zoo to
study animal taxonomy. They were to record: Kingdom, Phylum,
Class, Order, Family, Genus, and Species. But, the only thing they
were really learning was how to copy down information. They were
supposed to work together in groups of four, but she straggled
behind. She didn't want the caged animals associating her with the
others. She didn't want the animals staring at her, thinking she was
part of the group that was taunting, pointing, and laughing. She
pressed her hand to the window.

"I'm sorry," Violet whispered to the gorillas.

After her group copied the information from the plaque, they checked their hair in their faint reflections of the display glass and then scurried off as though they had a race to win. Violet stood there quietly watching the apes. She was guilty for intruding on their lives. She wrote: Animalia, Chordata, Mammalia, Primates, Hominidae, Gorilla, G. *beringei.*

She headed slowly towards the marine exhibit. She didn't hear the kids shouting or the cars that passed outside the mountain façade that stretched around the perimeter of the park. All she could hear was her breathing. When she arrived, her attention was immediately caught by the polar bears swimming as if they were dancing in slow motion. The public pool at the end of her street was larger than the one the bears had.

"They look like they rolled in dirt," Violet said to nobody, as she wrote: Animalia, Chordata, Mammalia, Carnivora, Ursidae, Ursus, *U.maritimus.*

On the bus ride home her stomach began to hurt. It was as though a strong fist was pulling on her insides, but she took comfort in being warm, bundled in her green parka wearing white ear muffs and black Magic Mini gloves her mother had bought at Canadian Tire.

That night Violet and her family gathered around the television to watch *La Bamba*: the tragic story of Ritchie Valens.

"This is the music I grew up with. He was one of the other guys who got killed with Buddy Holly," her father proudly exclaimed.

Her father was five years old the day the music died.

Their TV room was like a watering hole in the Serengeti; from time to time it was a place to rest, but you always had to be on guard. At the end of the film, there was a slow-motion montage of Ritchie at various points of his life while his brother screamed out his name: "Riiitchieee!" Violet wanted to cry with Ritchie's brother, but she couldn't until she was alone. Her family would have turned on her. She would have been the sickly zebra (Animalia, Chordata, Mammalia, Perissodactyla, Equidae, Equus, *E. quagga*) separated from the herd. Violet got up.

"Where are *you* going?" Stanley asked.

Violet didn't answer. She got to the washroom just in time for the lump in her throat to explode as she pushed in the lock and turned on the faucet to drown out the sniffling. Violet fumbled with her zipper and then rolled her jeans down to her shaking knees as she sat on the toilet. As Violet rubbed her eyes with the back of her hand, a metallic scent filled the room.

She bent over and wiped front to back. A rusty tint soaked through the white tissue.

⌘⌘⌘

A year before, Violet had come home to find a mysterious book on her pillow. She skimmed past the marked chapter on budding breasts and widening hips and, instead of focusing on becoming a woman, Violet became engrossed with the chapter on erections and nocturnal emissions.

Violet would race home every day after school to read that chapter and didn't pay much attention to anything else. One day the book disappeared as magically as it had appeared.

Eventually, Violet and her mother took the training bra trip to Woodward's.

"Why couldn't I just find one on my pillow after school?" she thought as she fumbled with her hands on her lap.

"How's school?"

"Fine."

Her mother turned up the radio.

Violet Quesnel

Not only did she get a bra that day, her mother designed a survival kit for a girl who was about to become a woman: a stick of deodorant, a box of panty liners, and pink-handled razors. Her mother told her: "This is all you'll need."

⟿⟿⟿

So, there she sat with her jeans at her knees and the faucet running, staring at her panties. She thought about telling her mother. But, by not telling anyone, it didn't really happen. After all, she still hadn't worn the bra. Only sometimes. At night. When she was in bed. She'd pretend that her boyfriend, who didn't exist, would try to take it off, but he wouldn't be successful because "no means no" and she was saving herself for marriage. Instead of wearing the bra Violet would wear layers, even in the sweat of July. Lucille, her grandmother who watched Violet and her siblings after school because Violet's mother went back to work, found the stained panties.

"You should have soaked them, dear."

Her grandmother removed the stain with borax. Violet avoided her grandmother's glance as she took the panties and placed them in the top right-hand drawer with the mismatched socks and the bra that also didn't exist. Days later her grandmother was admitted to the psychiatric ward. Violet blamed her stained panties.

⟿⟿⟿

Violet wasn't allowed to visit her grandma. When Violet's mother went to visit, Lucille thought her daughter was her old friend Gwendolyn. Gwendolyn and Lucille used to trade recipes and secrets in the small drilling town, especially when their men were in the fields.

"Gwen, don't you think my hair is growing in nicely?"

There was no evidence of a bald spot as her fingers twirled and twirled through her thick curly locks. She kept twirling as she stared through her daughter's eyes. Turns out Lucille's husband had ripped her hair from her scalp decades before. She was protecting her son from being thrown down the stairs.

It was memories like this that finally took a toll on her grandmother. The report said she was found at the University train station in a housecoat wearing only one slipper and carrying a green suitcase. Perhaps, no one would have noticed her if she hadn't tripped and fallen down the escalator. Her nose started bleeding and through sobs she whispered over and over that she wouldn't have time to get the blood out of her clothing before Reginald got home.

Violet got to see her grandmother months later, when Lucille was discharged from the hospital. While Lucille was in the kitchen getting water for her medication, Violet sat in the living room looking at the décor. Above the kitchen entrance a wreath made out of plastic forks and lace hung unevenly. It somehow made sense next to the row of anniversary plates that her grandmother had collected from estate sales. Violet was most intrigued by a wooden reindeer next to the old rabbit-eared television set that had a vice grip in place of a tuning knob. The reindeer had a Mason jar for its belly and was filled with melted ribbon candy. A reindeer in the middle of wet May.

"Would you like one, dear?" Her grandmother pointed to the jar.

The girl managed a smile and shook her head. She walked over to her grandmother and gave her a hug. Over her grandmother's shoulder, Violet noticed a black and white photograph hiding behind a pile of "Get Well Soon" cards. She'd never seen this picture before. Violet went to the photograph and traced the outline of the frame with her finger.

"That's our engagement photo, dear."

In the photograph Lucille and Reginald are smiling. Reginald's arms are behind his back. Lucille's are wrapped around his waist and what Lucille hasn't learned yet is that nothing will change from that moment on. She will forever hold on to him even after he beats her, even after he remarries, even after his death.

◦◦◦◦

In Violet's closet there was an open box of panty liners. She didn't want her mother to know her secret. Nothing good ever came out of being a woman. One night her mother called her into the laundry room. Her mother stood there with the open box in her one hand, her other hand on her hip.

"Did you get your period?"

Violet nodded. Her mother looked like Violet did earlier, when she placed the liner adhesive on her pubic hair instead of on the crotch of her panties. She felt ashamed that her mother knew because bleeding only meant trouble. Her mother just stared through Violet.

"Why didn't you tell me?"

Violet shrugged, walked to her room, and turned up the radio.

The Certificate

WHEN THE NEWS WEAVED THROUGH THE family grapevine, the hens began clucking overtime. There was plenty of shock and concern but Violet never heard about it directly. That's the thing about family shame; it's too much to deal with directly. It wasn't easy living together. Violet plus her family equalled a toxic combination. So even though Violet didn't want to stay with them, she needed a place to live.

Up until this point it had been difficult for Violet to understand why she was put on earth because of the bombardment of distractions. The traffic. The media. The mission for the perfect mate. She realized that she could no longer avoid reality curled-up in a drowsy haze. She had discovered that a baby was growing inside of her and this inspired her to keep moving.

The guarded interactions at her parents' house grew tiresome. It was just like the good ol' days. Violet was comfortable with being the topic of the day, but she grew restless. She made her way west to Calgary to live with her uncle and his family. Along the way a suitcase of Violet's belongings was snatched from the bed of the truck.

For reasons only obvious to those who knew her, Violet wasn't able to hold a job. No job; no money. She attended interviews but there was never a follow-up call. She vaguely understood why no one would want to hire an obviously pregnant woman with dry skin and swollen fingers. She had no other choice but to apply for social assistance. Ah, pregnancy — such a beautiful time in a woman's life, such a happy time. The scrutiny of the application process was wrenching. They asked for the name of the father.

"I don't know who the father is." Violet said.

So now not only was Violet an unemployed, mentally ill, pregnant woman, she was loose. A tramp. Slut. She never gave Jason's name. Not to protect him but to protect her from what she could only assume to be a difficult situation. She didn't want to think about the future dealing with custody and financial support matters. She didn't want Jason testifying: "She's unfit!"

Violet filled out Sophia's birth certificate application as follows:

FATHER'S NAME: ——————

FATHER'S PLACE OF BIRTH: ——————

Even though Violet's pregnancy was swiftly being accessorized with a pretty big bow of red tape, she felt terrific. No more nausea, with the exception of chicken because the aroma of poultry cooking smelled like decomposition. For the first time in ages her thoughts were rational and her emotions were in check. She was able to sleep; she mainly drank fruit drinks and ate microwavable pizza.

For kicks, Violet looked up Pierce's number in the phone book. She hadn't heard from him since his visit to Sault Ste. Marie. She wasn't sure where he was living or if he was still in the Forces.

There on the page: Rezek, P.

"Hey, it's Violet. I'm living in Calgary. Maybe we could meet for lunch or something. Gimme a call."

Pierce called later that evening.

"You've returned," he said.

"When can we meet?" she asked.

She met Pierce downtown at the Olympic Plaza train station. She wanted to kiss him.

"Your hair is longer," he said

"It's been awhile since I've seen you. Hair grows."

They walked, ate shawarma, and walked some more. They concluded their journey at Devonian Gardens. The indoor garden air was heavy and humid on that brisk November afternoon.

They had found each other again.

"I'm pregnant," she said.

Pierce stopped and hugged her. "I'm so excited for you!"

Pierce entertained Violet throughout her pregnancy. They'd go for walks, she'd watch him drink beers at the St. Louis Hotel and play pool with this friends. When her stomach blocked the view of her feet, he'd tie her shoes and clip her toe nails.

"You're going to be a great mother, Violet."

Everything was progressing as well as could be expected.

After being awake for over twenty-four hours in unspeakable pain, laced with multiple shots of Demerol and acquiring a new nitrous oxide dependency, Violet becomes hysterical. Janet isn't much help, spending most of her time in the corner of the room crying into the arms of her comic-book-reading, WWF-loving, concert-T-shirt-wearing boyfriend. They'd been together for a couple years. Janet has been hoping for this to be The One; however, come autumn she'll have a stroke and he won't believe there's anything wrong with her. Going to work, he'll leave Janet in the shower lying in her own shit; water running down her left-side. Numb. Alone.

Before long, Sophia Francis Quesnel's head crowns and she is pushed into the world.

pushpushpushpush

Violet looks at the photograph of her and Sophia together after she is born — blood and mucus smeared on the baby's face:

I look happy.

This bliss is short lived.

Extreme postpartum depression rears its ugly head.

"Don't worry!" encouraged her physician. "It is not uncommon for women to hear babies crying when there are no babies crying around them."

What wasn't normal: the intrusive thoughts that people wanted to hurt the baby. People were plotting to suffocate Sophia. Violet was convinced. She kept watch constantly. She lost sleep because of her vigilance.

During the baby shower Violet spent most of the time crying. She was a train wreck of a mother holding the precious Sophia, while guests sat smiling next to them. Violet refused to take the prescribed medication to help her sleep and to ease the intruding thoughts of someone hurting Sophia; she was determined to keep breastfeeding. Violet didn't want to poison her daughter.

"Violet, you need to start taking medication," instructed Dr. Brown.

"No. I need to give my baby the best start in life."

"If you don't take the medication, you'll have to be hospitalized."

Where this all began.

Violet fills the prescription.

Knowing her daughter watches her every movement is enough to persuade Violet to shower and to use toothpaste. Violet's inner noises of despair have been replaced with squeals of delight, but as Sophia grows older and begins to gain independence Violet's mind will start to waiver.

Trumpet

January 5, 1993
Violet,

   It's a new year and life is great! Not because of what's
happening around me but because I am dealing with things
in a more positive way. I've been reading more, (by the way I
haven't read any Coleridge) and finding that I'm more open to
things I would judge in the past. I know that everything in my
past has brought me to this point and now I'm going to try hard
to not let it distract me from right now. I hope you don't think
I'm messed up because you're the first person I've opened up to
about this new me. I know I'll have my skeptics . . .

THE HONK OF THE 6:00 AM Greyhound out of Edmonton
interrupted my reading as it pulled into the garage. I folded the
letter, slipped it into the bulky envelope, placed my rucksack in
the compartment under the bus, and found an empty seat. I sat my
trumpet case on the seat next to me and stuffed the manila envelope
inside my jacket. I was nervous about packing the envelope with the
rest of my things just in case my luggage went missing.

⋘⋙

Heading east on Highway 16A, I was lucky to have a couple of
seats to myself, but as the bus continued, more and more people got
on — some with luggage, some without. I stared out the window
trying not to think about how itchy my face felt. It had been a
couple of days since I shaved. At Vegreville, I spotted the pysanka.

These small towns have the most bizarre "world's largest" attractions: the sausage coil, the sturgeon, the hockey stick, the apple, the Indian head, the tipi. When we passed the pysanka, I noticed a family of six, with a dog squirming in the father's arms, trying to pose in front of the Ukrainian Easter egg. The last time my family posed for a picture was before my parents divorced. We were on a summer road trip from Calgary to Vancouver and back. Dad thought it would be "neat" if we stopped at the Hope Slide. My brother and I were excited thinking that we would get to play on Canada's largest slide. What he failed to tell us was that it was a devastating landslide where people had died. I remember my father laughed at us.

When the bus driver opened the door, a woman with a black and gold jacket got on the bus. I tried not to make eye contact because she looked like a talker. She shuffled her way down the aisle and stopped right beside me. She smiled and nodded towards my trumpet. I gave in and moved it to the overhead compartment so she could sit down.

"Excuse me, you dropped something."

The envelope.

"Thanks."

I tried to keep my answers short and simple because I wasn't in the mood to talk, but my efforts to mind my own business fell short. I even pretended that I was reading *The Complete Poetical Works of Samuel Taylor Coleridge*. Yet, I couldn't concentrate on the poems. I kept reading over and over again:

Water, water, every where,
And all the boards did shrink;
Water, water, every where,
Nor any drop to drink . . .

"That looks like an interesting book."

I nodded.

Then she asked me where I was headed.

"Sault Ste. Marie."

"Oh, that's quite the trip! I'm just going as far as Kenora. Have you been to Kenora?"

I shook my head. I went back to my book, hoping she'd take the hint; however, it was no use. Her persistence reminded me of Violet.

"My parents live there. Who are you going to see?"

I felt guilty as hell trying to ignore her. She was harmless and I got the feeling she really needed someone to talk to. She had dark brown eyes with gold flecks. I figured it would be easier to indulge her at the moment and then maybe she'd be quiet the rest of the way.

"A friend," I replied.

"The tone in your voice suggests this is more than a 'friend'. Tell me more."

❧❧❧

I first received the desperate call to visit Violet in Sault Ste. Marie about three years ago, but I was just starting the second year of my degree — time and money were scarce. I felt horrible that I couldn't be there for her, and I think she felt snubbed because I had to wait longer in between letters, but now I am less than one day, twenty-two hours and thirty minutes away from delivering her mail.

You see, we met about seven years ago . It was election night at Junior Achievement and I didn't want to run for any executive positions because I figured I'd lose to the boisterous girl who wore cardigans and canvas sneakers. She was always smiling and friendly with everyone. She was the only member who believed in our product — a plain black box with a battery-operated mechanism inside so that when you inserted a loony into the slot it would buzz.

I thought the idea was ridiculous and I knew I couldn't compete with her optimism. On this particular night she sat down next to me and smiled.

"I'm Violet." She adjusted her ponytail and tilted her head. "You are?"

"Pierce."

"So, are you running for a position?"

"I was thinking of president, but I don't have a speech prepared." I was really only there to meet girls because I was growing bored with the usual suspects like members of the cheerleading squad or student council. I was tired of hanging out with the girls I was supposed to be with.

"How about: 'My name's Pierce. Vote for me because I'm nice.'"

I laughed. *She* was nice.

I recited her line and won, which wasn't difficult because I had no competition. I decided I had to ask her out. She was amazing at the meetings, speaking to each member and the mentors, smiling and being genuinely interested in what they had to say. She'd hover between people like a helicopter taking establishing shots like the ones at the beginning of *Dallas*. But when I saw her at school or on the train, she would be very quiet and solemn and she'd usually be reading.

To celebrate the end of the Junior Achievement year, our company went on a tour of Alberta's largest electrical company, our corporate sponsor, and we met with some big wig in a cold boardroom. It was our reward. He spoke with us about business and the future of young entrepreneurs and then he asked if there were any questions. We were fifteen — what were we supposed to ask? Violet knew.

"So, what do you think about Mulroney and this GST business?"

The room became still after everyone turned and stared at her. There had been whispers about how the government was going to implement a federal sales tax next year. I was embarrassed for her because I was only comfortable with attention when it was at a distance, like when I was in a scrum on the rugby pitch or the time my photo made the local sports page in the *Calgary Herald*. But now, the attention on her was at arms' length and the mood in the room became very uneasy. A couple of people snickered as they turned to the TransAlta corporate officer to see his reaction, but he simply unfolded his arms and replied, "That's a very good question." Violet sat there looking pleased with herself as she and the big guy continued their conversation about the Conservatives as if no one else was in the room.

⊷⊷⊷

The bus driver's voice interrupted, "Ten-minute break in North Battleford."

The lady grabbed her lighter and a cigarette from her coat. "I'll be right back and then you can tell me why you watched *Dallas*."

"I'm sorry, I didn't catch your name," I said.

"Gloria. I'll be right back and then you can tell me why you watched *Dallas*."

"I watched it with my mother when I was a kid. I'll save your spot, Gloria."

⊷⊷⊷

At the spring dance, Violet stood out because she was wearing a formal dress — which was odd considering it was a casual high school event. For once her hair wasn't pulled back in a ponytail, instead it curled around her face. She was out of breath, dancing alone in the middle of the gym, but she didn't seem to mind. I heard people whispering and saw them nodding towards her. I went to talk to her anyway. She smelled like warm baby powder and her eyes reflected the different coloured lights that spun on the DJ's table. I think I asked her to a basketball game.

"How about if we make Jell-O instead?"

Violet was always restless and would say such bizarre things. I really didn't know how to talk with her or how to approach her because every time we saw each other she was different. It seemed like one minute she was really into what I was saying and the next minute it was like she was the only one in the room. There would be days when I wouldn't hear from her or even see her in the halls. I started to think that she didn't care about me or that she was seeing someone else; I mean it wasn't long ago that sort of thing happened with my parents. Violet's absence made me uneasy so I gave up on her.

⊸⊸⊸

"We have about a four-hour layover in Saskatoon. Would you like some company for lunch?" asked Gloria.

"I think I'd like some time to myself."

Gloria looked hurt. I didn't know what to say so I didn't say anything.

I walked down 23rd Street to the Meewasin Trail. I was trying to find a quiet place on the riverbank to play the trumpet. I didn't really want an audience; I just needed inspiration for the next 2247 kilometres.

One day I hope to play with the RCA Jazz Sextet. Right now there's no room for me so until then I only play with the reed and brass ensemble. In my spare time I mess around with songs like "So What" by Miles Davis or "Salt Peanuts" by Dizzy Gillespie. I'll never be as cool, or as smooth as those masters, but how cool can you be in camouflage? There's not much room for riffing in the army. I found a sunny spot on the riverbank. A few cyclists sped past. It was good to stretch my legs and my lips with the sun on my face and the breeze carrying the notes along the South Saskatchewan River.

Back on the bus, Gloria said to me:

"Hey, there's an empty seat near the back; do you want me to move?"

"No, the bus will probably fill up in Regina." I didn't want to start all over with someone new.

"Oh, I just thought that — "

"You are fine where you are — promise."

We both breathed and then smiled.

"Where did you go on your walk?"

"Along the river, I went off the path. The riverbank was difficult to maneuver with my trumpet, but we made it." I gently tapped the trumpet case and smiled.

One day Violet came to my door.

"Where have you been?" I asked.

"Around," she motioned with a sweeping circular hand gesture.

"I didn't think I'd ever hear from you again, Violet."

"My parents bought a CD player. Do you want to go for a walk?"

We headed out with no destination in mind. Violet always put her hands in her pockets. It had begun to rain, so we cut through the golf course. It had been some time since a girl wouldn't let me kiss her. I liked kissing because then there was no talking. I was always so worried about saying the wrong thing; not speaking was easier than sounding stupid. I touched her hips when I helped her over the fence. She seemed very uneasy about getting her feet wet so I comforted her by holding her hand and then by lending her a pair of socks when we got to my house. She told me she remembered being born. I didn't really get it when she started describing her memory, but I didn't really get most things she talked about. Instead of showing my ignorance, I led her to the den.

"I rented a movie — *Friday the 13ᵗʰ Part VIII: Jason Takes Manhattan*," I said.

"I can't watch it."

"Why?"

"I'll have nightmares. Do you think Jason will take Berlin in part nine?" she asked.

Other girls would have watched the movie so I could put my arms around them when they got scared. Not Violet. She refused to watch horror films; instead I played with the remote control as she fidgeted with the drapes. Her father was going to pick her up soon. We walked to the front hall, and after she tied her shoelaces, she slowly stood up and that was when I pulled her towards me and kissed her. Back then I thought I was a good kisser, but I also wished every song on the radio was a Tragically Hip song.

⤙⤙⤙

In Regina, Gloria asked, "Would you like to have coffee with me?"

"You must be getting bored with listening to me."

We continued making small talk in the depot coffee shop. She wanted to go outside for another cigarette. We walked up Hamilton Street to check out the SaskPower building.

"I think it's shaped like an 'S'."

Gloria nodded in agreement as she deeply inhaled.

The silence was kind of nice.

As we walked back to the depot, I explained to Gloria that it was after the third month of dating that I think Violet started to feel more comfortable around me. She'd let me hold her hand in public and she had started twirling my curly hair around her finger when we watched television. Unfortunately, one day I answered the door and there on the stoop was Violet crying. She told me she had to move to Sault Ste. Marie.

"My dad . . . his job. A new school."

I stood there watching as her face grew redder. She couldn't look me in the eyes any longer. I grabbed her shirt and pulled her to me. All the kissing in the world didn't fix the problem because a month later she moved away.

⇆⇆⇆

It had been a long day by the time we re-boarded. The quiet whispers turned into a hum of sleeping travellers, but I couldn't sleep. I kept thinking about Violet.

I received letters from Violet every two weeks or so. She'd mainly write about what she was reading. Her words on the page seemed so enthusiastic that she inspired me to read books that I didn't have to. Because of her, I didn't need to be the president of a company, the rugby star, or even the boyfriend. None of that impressed her.

I wanted to tell Violet I was working on my undergrad at the University of Calgary majoring in musical performance. I'd played the trumpet in junior high band but took a hiatus to play sports in high school because it wasn't considered "cool" in my circle of friends to be in band. I was taking private lessons; nobody knew except my mother. Violet was the inspiration. She was always going on about art and how it "moved" her. It was mainly books she loved, and it was this love that added something different to my ordinary existence. I wasn't consumed any longer about the "big play" or the party that everyone was going to; playing the trumpet helped me think about nothing but playing the trumpet.

After high school, I didn't know what to do with my life. I didn't want to wear a suit every day, sitting in boardrooms devoid of personality. Violet always said, "I don't understand why people are motivated by money or vengeance. We should do things in life for love."

Gloria woke me up in Winnipeg. But we didn't talk; we just walked around the depot. It was a needed break. When we got back on the bus, Gloria squeezed my hand and said, "So, tell me more about this girl."

It was easy to talk to Gloria. She was actually interested in what I had to say.

⟨⊸⟩⟨⊸⟩⟨⊸⟩

Violet's enthusiasm for art was contagious. During my time at the U of C, I played in local clubs with small-time bands. After graduation, I wanted to do something that mattered, something that had more daily structure than playing in smokey clubs until 3:00 AM and staggering home with the latest groupie. Sure, it was great at first being hit on by many women and the occasional man because I was a musician, but it quickly turned flat. I sent in my audition tape to the Royal Canadian Artillery Band stationed in Edmonton. If I got accepted, not only would I have to give a live audition, I would embark on thirteen weeks of basic training — weapons, survival, army policy and procedures — a swirl of discipline and creativity. In June 1996, I became Private Rezek.

I was now serving my country as an artist.

⟨⊸⟩⟨⊸⟩⟨⊸⟩

"Here we are in the teeming metropolis of Kenora. I'd love to hear how things work out. I'd ask you to write, but . . . "

"Hey, Vegreville is only an hour bus trip away from Edmonton. We should go for coffee sometime."

"Sure, just in case things don't work out with Violet."

I smiled as Gloria hopped off the bus and embraced a great bear of a man.

For the rest of the trip I read. "Frost at Midnight" lulled me to sleep but I didn't dream of my birthplace or old church towers, I dreamed about Violet. I awoke and read "The Aeolian Harp" and nodded off again wondering what "soft floating witchery of sound" would actually sound like. I wondered how Violet would describe the sound of my trumpet and I thought about what I would say to her. I don't think we ever settled the score. Soon after she moved away, she found out I was dating her friend. She thought that we were still together even though the distance kept us apart. I fogged the window with my breath and drew a face with a frown with my finger tip.

When I arrived in the Soo, (I think that is what Violet called it), I found a payphone. Janet answered.

"Hi, it's Pierce. I'm at the bus depot by the Algonquin Hotel. Labatt Blue neon sign in the window."

"Violet doesn't live here anymore."

"Do you know where she is?"

When Janet arrived, I jumped into her pick-up truck and placed the book on the dash.

"So why the hell are you in Ontario?" she asked. "When did you start reading?"

I told her about how Violet would write me letters and suggest writers I should read. She was on a big Coleridge kick awhile back. "She'd go on and on about genius."

"She was in the hospital, you know," said Janet.

I also explained how Violet desperately wanted me to come visit her when she called me.

⊷⊷⊷

"Hello, Pierce? It's Violet."

"Where are you?" I asked.

"In the kitchen."

"I can't believe you're calling me."

[44]

"Has it been that long? You should visit," suggested Violet.

"Where are you, Vi?"

"The Soo."

"I can't fly out."

"You can't write letters either. Take the bus then. I'd really like to see you. Please. We'll go dancing. Remember how much fun we had dancing?" Violet said.

"I remember how much fun *you* had dancing."

"So just like that? You aren't going to visit me? I was hoping you could come with me to Hamilton."

"What's in Hamilton, Violet?"

"I just need to get there."

I knew there was something wrong. She was excited at the beginning of the phone call, but by the end of our conversation, she was deflated. Her voice sounded shrivelled like a weeks-old birthday balloon that no one wanted to pop or throw away. She was hanging on the end of the telephone cord.

❦❦❦

"I remember her calling you. Shortly after that Mom and Dad *encouraged* her to be admitted, and then with the help of the hospital social worker, they found her a safe place to live. Semi-independent living I think they call it."

"Will I be able to see her?"

I must have looked as guilty as I felt.

"It's not your fault, you know."

❦❦❦

"The envelope is filled with old cards and letters for you that I had never mailed. I was always worried that they weren't good enough to send, even though you'd keep writing me letters asking if I was in jail or dead. I figured you should know I tried. It's just a small stack of letters and Christmas and birthday cards as well as a Halloween card. See, it has a picture of a cat on the front with a text bubble that says 'Happy Halloween from the dog.' The punch line on the inside says, 'Pretty good costume, eh?' I figured you'd get a kick out of it."

The brown and orange crocheted blanket was pulled up to her chin. Her hair tied back in a ratty ponytail. She looked up at me from the couch.

"Will you read them to me?"

⟷⟷⟷

On my way back to CFB Edmonton, I wished Gloria had been on the bus. I wanted to tell her how Violet was just as pretty as the first time I met her. And about how we sat on the couch in her parents' den with her dog between us and watched Blacksploitation films for the jive talking and the fast cars. About how I read "Kubla Khan" out loud and tried to get her to eat. How I made her a pita, but she barely swallowed half of a half.

"Keep reading your letters to me."

. . . *to tell you the truth, Violet, I'm in a bit of a low mood today; I knew that if I didn't write you soon, it may be even harder later. It's not that I don't like writing to you, it's just that I don't know what to say. I have problems talking back and forth in person, and on paper I have no idea what I'm doing. I hope things are better. Are you on any medication right now? I miss you and I hope our paths cross again. I love the tape you made me. I have a new respect for Elvis. Don't lose touch.*

Love Pierce

Violet's face turned red as though she was moving away all over again. I reached out and held her hand and asked, "So, do you still want to go to Hamilton?"

Knitting

LUCILLE HESITATED TO WATCH HER GRANDCHILDREN after school when her daughter Judy decided to go back to work in 1986. Women didn't work outside the home in Lucille's day because there was so much to be done inside the home. She was in charge of clothing and feeding her seven children, the grocery shopping, making sure the eldest children got to school on time, and putting the younger ones down for their naps. Dinner had to be on the table before Reginald got home from the oil fields. She had to make beds, take the laundry off the lines, iron it, and then put it away. She had to leave enough time to put her make-up on and do her hair so she could look just right when she greeted him at the door with a rye and a smile. She tried to be a textbook example of a good wife, but the harder she tried, the harder it became to please Reggie. Now, would she be able to please Judy?

In 1951, Lucille was introduced to Reginald by her friend Gwen at a picnic celebrating the end of seeding around the Gull Lake area. The ground was dry and the wind was hot. Prairie soil complemented each bite of their chicken sandwiches by making the mayonnaise gritty. Half the plaid blanket Lucille was seated on kept lifting off the ground. It was difficult to enjoy her lunch when she had to keep attending to the blanket. Reginald sat down next to her.

"It looks like you need some help," he said.

He was tall with blonde hair that was combed into a pompadour. His ears stuck out proudly as they framed his smile.

They sat in silence and exchanged awkward glances as they finished their potato salad.

"Gwendolyn tells me you fought in the war," said Lucille.

"Would you like to go to the town dance with me?" Reginald asked.

In the background, a projector ticks and an image of two lovebirds dancing closely slowly flashes on the screen. Their granddaughter, Violet, will love watching them dance and will especially love it when Reginald dances with her. Her socks slide on linoleum while she tries to balance on the tops of his feet, dancing to the jaunty verse she will believe he wrote:

Down in the bootlegger cellar,
A tom cat chased a mouse.
A police dog came around the corner
And he had one on the house.

⊕⊕⊕

After a few more picnics, town hall dances, and moonlight drives to check the crops, Reginald proposed. Excited, Lucille stopped fidgeting with the strand of beads around her neck.

The tie he was wearing was tied too short and it got tangled in her necklace as they embraced.

They headed back to the home quarter where Reginald knew both families would be awaiting the announcement.

"Lucille and Reginald, come pose for a picture."

They are standing next to each other in front of the grain truck smiling. Reginald's arms are behind his back. Lucille's are wrapped around his waist and what Lucille hasn't learned yet is that nothing will change from that moment on. She will forever hold on to him.

⊕⊕⊕

On the first day babysitting, Lucille cleaned out the pantry and reorganized the cupboards; she set the table, cooked dinner, and ensured the television was off and that the kids were doing their homework. All of this fuss made her granddaughter Violet uneasy.

"Grandma, you don't have to do so much work. I'll set the table."

Violet thought she was being helpful, but instead she made Lucille anxious. Without realizing it, Violet was ordering her grandmother around and making her second-guess her position as caregiver. After about a month of vacuuming and scrubbing stains out of clothes, Lucille was found bleeding and rambling at the train station with a green suitcase and her left slipper missing.

Once in the hospital, Lucille repeatedly told the nurses and anyone else who would listen that she was going to be in trouble when he got home. Lucille's children were perplexed by her fear because Reginald and his new wife had moved away from the city. Clearly, Lucille was oblivious to reality, but finally, she was getting the care she deserved after all those years.

Reginald and Lucille's fourth child was born deformed. The doctor wouldn't let Lucille hold him. The baby was whisked away leaving her alone, frightened, and high on hormones.

Ryan lived for three days never knowing his mother's embrace or how his father's finger felt in the grasp of his tiny hand. Ryan was placed in a cedar box without ceremony, but there were tears — tears mixed with rage and rye. And so it began.

"You killed him," Reginald told Lucille.

As Reginald's depression terrorized the family, Lucille turned to the church for the unconditional love she wanted.

For many Christmases they wouldn't have a trimmed tree, but she would stay up all night to make the dinner and to wrap knitted socks. The only time Lucille could get anything done, even if it meant not getting enough sleep, was when Reginald was out drinking. As their other sons turned into teenagers, they would bring their father home with vomit on his shirt and asphalt on his face.

⊷⊷⊷

Gwen stopped by to see how Lucille was dealing with the loss of Ryan and how she was managing the other three children. Reginald and Gwen's husband, Frank, had left that morning to go to the drilling fields and would not be home for a few days.

"I had some of your sour cream pie at church yesterday. Do you think I could get your recipe?" Gwen said.

Lucille quietly swept the kitchen floor. "I don't have it written down."

"Do you have time to make one with me, Lucy? I'll take notes."

Lucille went to the cupboard and placed a bowl on the counter.

Gwen smelled the wild flowers showcased in a foggy milk bottle on the table. "These flowers are sure nice. Are they from Reg?"

Lucille slowly nodded.

"Is this a bad time, Lucy?"

"No, I'm glad you are here. I have a bit of a headache is all."

Gwen noticed a handful of hair in the dustpan as Lucille emptied it into the garbage.

"What's wrong, Lucille?"

"Reginald was drinking again and starting in on Samuel, 'No son of mine is going to wear short pants!' He grabbed Sam and was heading towards the stairs to change his clothes. I thought he might fall because he was so drunk and so I got in the middle and well . . . "

Lucille bent her head towards Gwen.

"Lucille — "

"It'll grow back, Gwen. Let's get started on the pie."

Memories like this and the new pressures of looking after Judy's kids built up in Lucille's mind; this led to her robe getting caught in the escalator causing her to trip at the station. She told the on-call psychiatrist why she needed to pack and to get as far away from her place as possible, but she couldn't find the children.

"I dreamt that I walked down to the carport and I looked into Reginald's old Dodge. It's light blue with white interior. There on the backseat was a dead body. A man with ghostly skin. Blood splattered on his face and on the seats. I start running in slow motion and I come to the side of the house and there by the chimney is a nest with broken robin's eggs. Baby blue egg shells and specks of blood. I woke up thinking that I wouldn't be able to get the mess cleaned up before he got home. He's going to be so angry. I told myself I had to get away and if I didn't fall I would have, but now he is going to find me."

"Lucille, do you know what day it is?"

"It's Tuesday."

"What year is it?"

"1968. Do you know where my children are?"

Years later when her granddaughter moved back to Calgary after living in Sault Ste. Marie, Violet went to visit Lucille because now she had something in common with her grandmother. After Reginald's death, Lucille was braver than she ever was when he was alive. She was able to speak her mind without worrying about consequences, but she'd still speak in a whisper just in case he could still hear her and would be waiting for her on the other side.

"He would drink himself blind and try to show your uncles what a real man was. He had a special relationship with a man from down the block. I suspect they were in love."

"Grandma, what about the time my mom was about twelve years old?" said Violet.

"I don't know what time you're asking about, dear."

"One time when Mom was visiting during my first admission to the hospital, she told me that she knew there was something wrong with you when she was awakened by a sound," said Violet.

"Your grandma had been canning chokecherry syrup earlier that morning before the house got too hot when the sun came out. When I woke up my mom was back in the kitchen still canning. But not berries. As I walked closer I noticed the counter lined with jars of grass and twigs, toy cars, and even her favourite strand of beads. Mom was just beginning to pour pectin into a jar with my father's car keys. She stopped when she saw me standing there and then turned up the radio and began dancing and laughing alone."

"She asked you what you were doing and you said you had to get things ready for Ryan's birthday party. Mom remembers helping you to your room and then she hid all the jars down in the basement."

"I don't remember."

Instead, Lucille remembered how she burned the letters Reginald wrote apologizing for hitting her, for his strict parenting style, and for getting remarried shortly after their divorce was final. (He needed someone to wash his clothes.) Years of alcoholism deteriorated both his body and mind and so Lucille chose to erase his memories contained in these letters by throwing the stack in the burning barrels behind her brother's abattoir. The letters went up in smoke along with the stench of decaying hooves and snouts.

"I took the brunt of his self-loathing," said Lucille.

꩜꩜꩜

Lucille wasn't the only one. Early one morning, Lucille had left her sleeping children and went to deliver some meals to the unmarried reverend. It was easy to slip out as Reginald hadn't been home in days. She cooked for Reverend Matthews out of duty to her church and because *he* never complained about her cooking. Then in 1993, Judy sat in a restaurant at a table eating a burger alone and Violet stood on the other side of the counter angry as hell. Angry for hearing the truth.

"How can she be so selfish thinking I'd be able to handle this," thought Violet.

Violet was beginning to pull away from Judy and the family. She wouldn't let Judy hug her anymore and she would spend hours in her room reading late at night when everyone else was asleep. One morning before the rest of the family was up, even before the sunrise, Judy heard a noise coming from the kitchen. There stood Violet making pizza.

"You're up early, Violet."

"I have to get this pizza in right away."

"Do you know what time it is?" asked Judy.

Violet shrugged as she flattened the dough on to the pizza stone. "Can you pass me the cheese?"

"I think you should go back to bed. You need your rest."

"No way, I'm not going back to that room."

"Why don't you want to go back to your room?" Judy held her breath.

Violet sat the pizza on the middle rack. She had arranged the sliced wieners and processed cheese slices in a happy face, but the ketchup made the pizza look like it was bleeding.

Judy never wanted her children to hurt like she did, yet here Violet stood picking dough from her rings at 5:00 AM looking like she was lost. Judy remembered why she didn't want to go back to her room when she was her daughter's age.

Violet sliced the pizza and offered her mother a piece. Judy declined. Violet had failed to turn the oven on and now she stared at the mess of dough and cheese and wieners and ketchup.

"I wasn't that hungry anyway," said Violet.

"Violet, there's something you should know."

Violet had never felt more helpless in her plight to be planted on even ground. Violet was having a hard enough time dealing with the inconsistent waves of emotions that swelled at the top of her stomach at the least appropriate moments. She couldn't look her mother in the eye. They didn't speak in the car when Judy drove Violet to work later that day. Nobody noticed that the radio wasn't on.

In the restaurant, Violet no longer recognized her mother.

The projector begins to tick again and the image of Judy as a girl, who was awakened by her father smelling of Old Spice and oil, blazes on the screen. Violet sees Judy struggling to free herself from Reginald's suffocating vehemence. His attempts are futile as he succumbs to his daughter's kicks and to the effects of alcohol. Judy was able to escape. Eventually, he comes to and in a haze he realizes where he is. He stumbles down the hall towards the kitchen to find his wide-eyed Judy at the table packing lunches for the children. Reginald says, "Your mother will die if you tell anyone." She had no reason to believe differently; there wasn't a day that went by when he didn't lay a hand on Lucille out of anger.

Judy confronted both her parents about that moment years later when she was a mother herself. In response, Reginald wrote a letter blaming the incident on a drinking blackout. This explanation will never be enough for Judy and it will certainly be unthinkable for Violet.

So, there Judy sat alone by the window as she unwrapped the foil from the burger Violet made for her. Staring straight ahead she bit into the sourdough bun and the mayonnaise stuck to the corners of her mouth.

It was difficult to talk about Reginald, the grandfather who bought ice cream on Sundays and helped put his grandchildren's toys together on Christmas Day, when the monster of the past overshadowed Lucille's and Judy's memories. Indeed this darker version of Reginald surprised Violet, for she only remembered him telling her funny stories about the war like how when he left his post to relieve himself in a raspberry bush and he ended up on KP duty, or how he learned to ride a bicycle for the first time outside London.

❧❧❧

"Reginald had demons," said Lucille.

"How can you forgive him, Grams?"

"Jesus forgives, Violet."

"But look at what you went through and your children — my mother . . ."

"I did the best I knew how. You'll understand one day."

Then Lucille handed Violet a pair of knitted booties.

Wet Socks

She told him she remembers being born. She forgot that she told him but he remembered and asked her about it years later when they met again in Calgary. Pierce was on leave visiting his mom.

"You remember being born, right?"

She paused for a moment, embarrassed because he had paid attention to her story.

"I didn't tell you that? Did I?" She scrunched up her nose.

"It isn't true?" Pierce asked.

"No, it's true; it's just that my memories are growing fainter."

He rolled his shoulders back and adjusted the straps on his knapsack.

"Why would you remember me telling you that?" she asked.

"You're the only person I know crazy enough to admit it. What was it like, again?" he teased.

"Never mind." Violet raised her eyebrows as she took a final gulp of her milkshake and then searched around the Brentwood train station for a garbage can.

"Violet, the train is here."

They found a seat in silence. She stared out the window and watched the university pass by. She does remember being born.

⊷⊷⊷

Ten years ago, Pierce and Violet met at a Junior Achievement meeting. Pierce joined to be president of a company and to meet girls. Violet joined to make her father proud. Pierce wasn't much of a president and Violet didn't seem to mind. They began dating. Violet had never had a boyfriend before, but he had dated plenty. Her stomach would churn at the thought of him. His dark eyes grew bigger when he smiled. She would get clammy hands around him and when he stood next to her she could feel the heat rising from his body. She always told him to kiss her — in her head, because the thought of an actual kiss was too much for her to bear. She'd fill the awkward silences between them with nervous stories, continually gesturing with her hands so he wouldn't be able to reach out and hold one of them.

One day it began raining as they were on a walk. That day Pierce thought it would be better to cut through the golf course because the moist sprinkle was turning into a heavy downpour. Violet thought she was going to pass out when he pushed up on her hips to ease her over the fence. On the other side she landed in a puddle and soaked her canvas sneakers and the bottoms of her jeans. She tried to wipe her shoes dry in vain before Pierce made it over. He scaled the fence with the ease of a cat and landed without a splash. He looked down and apologized for getting her feet wet, as he pulled her hand from her coat pocket and took it in his. There was mud and grass between their fingers.

When they arrived back at his house he led her to his room. She stood in the doorway wondering if her feet smelled as bad as she thought they did. He went to his dresser drawer.

"You should get out of those wet socks," he suggested. She wondered if his mom was home as she sat down on his bed and changed into the grey wool socks he gave her. She would never give them back. He stood leaning against his dresser just watching her — so she blurted out, "I remember being born."

Pierce smiled and crossed his arms.

"I do," insisted Violet.

"Oh? What was it like?"

He humoured her in the hopes that he'd be able to get to kiss her today. After all, they'd been going for walks for two months now and today was the first day that she let him hold her hand. Usually on their walks, or alternately while watching television, she'd look to the ground and talk about hockey or evolution or how her family was too much sometimes. She liked the evening news and "Bat Out of Hell" and Elvis Presley before his movie career, and after his weight gain, so when she said she remembered being born he wasn't that surprised.

"It was dark and then there was light."

"That's original," Pierce said.

"When it was dark it sounded like when you dive deep underwater . . . and then when I emerged the sound was crisp and the light . . . Shut your eyes. See the different colours on the inside of your lids? There were purples and yellows and greens moving in orbs just like that. Dark and then light. I was under water, and then I was free."

"Let's go watch TV."

He sat on the couch and motioned for her to join him.

"I don't like Brussels sprouts," she declared. She started twirling her damp hair around her finger.

"What do you want to watch?" Pierce pressed the remote.

She could feel warmth radiating off his thigh seconds away from hers.

"Where's your mom?" she asked.

"Working, I think." He put the remote down and turned towards hers. She could feel him staring at her.

"What time is it?" She searched for a clock.

Pierce cleared his throat.

"My dad is picking me up soon. I should be ready when she gets here."

"I like your smile." He reached over and touched her hand for the second time.

Violet looked at her feet tapping at the floor. "We're getting call waiting," she said.

She reached behind the couch and opened the curtain a touch. "It's stopped raining. I should get ready to go."

She walked to the foyer. Pierce followed. They stood waiting, not knowing the time. All Violet could hear was Pierce chewing his gum between heavy breaths. The space between them was the smallest it had ever been. She smelled cologne and wet shoes and mint. She felt her face burning. He reached out and grasped her sweatshirt and pulled her to him.

"Maybe my dad was in an accident?" she whispered.

Her eyes darted back and forth as she tried to avoid making eye contact. It was too late. His lips were pressed against hers. She didn't know what to do. His tongue filled her mouth with saliva and mint. The breathing sounds became muffled. The light made room for the dark underneath her lids. Everything seemed to stop.

⊹⊹⊹

A recording rang overhead: "The Calgary Zoo."

She had forgotten that she told him she remembered being born — him of all people.

"Here, let me get the door for you." Pierce pushed the button and the door slid open.

He was her first love and her first betrayal. They stood on the train platform for a moment as he adjusted his knapsack.

"When was the last time you were at the zoo?"

"Ages ago," Violet said.

She could feel him staring at her. She looked up from the ground and met his gaze.

"It's good to see you again. I wonder if your baby will remember."

She shrugged and touched her belly as they walked towards the entrance booth.

No More Tears

VIOLET SECURED SOPHIA INTO HER BOOSTER seat after picking her up from daycare.

"Hurry home, Mommy. I'm going to Esther's after dinner," said Sophia.

"I don't think so. I'm tired. I've been at work and then school since eight o'clock this morning. I still need to make dinner, and you need to have a bath tonight. Maybe you can go to her house on the weekend some time."

"But I told her I was coming over."

"You didn't ask me first to see if it would be okay. So you can call her when we get home and let her know you can play on the weekend," said Violet.

Sophia's tear-filled eyes quickly turn from a muted hazel to a vibrant green. This happened whenever she was angry. She crossed her arms over her chest and started kicking the glovebox. She hated hearing the word *no* but not because she never heard the word, but because when she got an idea in her head she expected it to play out exactly how she thought it should happen. Violet didn't know where she got that from.

"Sophia Francis Quesnel! I've told you before to make sure it's all right with me before you make plans. You're not the boss. Stop kicking!"

Sophia continued to kick the glovebox and started screaming at the top of her lungs.

"You're the worst mother in the world! You never let me play with my friends!"

Violet was grateful the windows were closed.

God, I hate when she screams. Why does she have to be so dramatic?

"Sophie, why are you acting this way. Now, you're definitely not going to Esther's."

They pulled up to the house they rented. It was built in the 1940s, was renovated into three suites, and was now in need of love. The grey paint was chipping off and the orange Spanish-style roof made Violet gag every time she saw it. The gutters needed to be cleaned out and the front entrance door, painted red, never closed properly. The house slanted to the left side in the front; Sophia's crayons placed on the coffee table would roll off immediately. The upper and main floors were cut in half and there was a basement suite where a man with a boasting laugh and a filthy mouth brought different women home now and then. The family living in the right suite were quiet. You wouldn't know someone lived there if it weren't for their dog.

Sophia refused to get out of the vehicle. Waiting for her daughter was interfering with Violet's plans to relax. She was tempted to leave Sophia in the car but Violet didn't trust the alley behind their place because people scavenged through the dumpsters daily. As she stood there, Violet noticed a freshly sprayed *Fuck You* on the dumpster. It was a nice addition to the neighbourhood although Violet would have used red paint instead of black. Sophia finally got out of the car, slammed the door, and then proceeded to let the block know what an awful parent Violet was:

"I hate you! You're so mean!"

Violet's patience was wearing thin. Inside the house, she sent Sophia to her room. Violet could hear her crying and yelling to her stuffed animals about how her plans were foiled by her evil mother.

Violet ignored her daughter's protests by turning on the black and white five-inch television that only picked up one channel and then she started making dinner. Cooking was a perfect activity to avoid painful circumstances. It could be the tingling sensations that travelled from her wrist, through her arm to her spine when a knife blade slid back and forth through a ripe tomato or perhaps it was the rhythmic sound of chopping celery on a wooden cutting board. Violet sometimes didn't like how aromas carried her to another time and place.

Whenever she walked past the PQ and PR stacks in the university library, it smelled like the second floor, east wing of the hospital with half-eaten food trays and clean sheets. The aroma reminded her of the body temperature/blood pressure machine, tears, and ankle/wrist restraints. Violet could hear the mantra: "It's for their safety and for ours." She remembered Dixie cups of water and multi-coloured pills, anorexics, meth heads, payphones for patient use only, the beginning bars of "Für Elise" played over and over again in the patient lounge, bumming cigarettes and drawing with pastels. It smelled like loneliness.

"Yes, cooking dinner is a good choice," Violet tried to convince the boiling water.

Sophia didn't know how to let things go. She made her way down the stairs; stomping her feet and banging her fists against the railing. She turned the corner and yelled at her mother.

"Fuck! Give me the phone so I can call Esther!" Did she just say *fuck?* The scorching contempt in her voice made Violet uneasy.

"Sophia! You're coming with me!" said Violet.

Violet dropped a lid onto the stove, grabbed Sophia's arm, and dragged her up the stairs. Her daughter did not go easily or quietly. She gave all that she had.

"No, Mom! Don't squeeze my arm so tight!"

"Quit fighting me, Sophia!"

"If you would . . . just let me go . . . to Esther's . . . !"

The struggle continued onto the next landing. It was difficult to get Sophia to let go of the banister. Violet stepped over a pile of dirty clothes at the top and while trying to avoid being sucked into this black hole of cotton-poly blend, her foot is pierced by a sharp object — Barbie's hand.

Confounded, plastic bitch!

They arrived at the bathroom and Sophia's eyes turned from scorching emeralds into stunned, black pools of dismay. She had heard the tales about her foul-mouthed aunties getting their mouths washed out with soap before, but Sophia never thought it would happen to her. Violet reached for the baby shampoo. It's non-toxic: how damaging could it be? Violet pried Sophia's mouth open and began to pour. Sophia spit at her mother and struggled to get away but Violet was quicker and stronger than her.

The deed was done.

Sophia was left in the bathroom alone to think about why it had to come to that moment.

No More Tears was a lie.

Violet, disgusted with herself, hesitated, and then walked down the stairs to continue making dinner. Violet didn't hear Sophia slink back into the kitchen because she was hypnotized by the hum of the microwave oven thawing chicken. Out of the corner of her eye she caught a glimpse of her daughter's shoulders moving up and down as Sophia tried to control her breathing. Violet turned to face her. Sophia stood glaring at Violet. Bubbles foamed around her puckered mouth as she said: "I hope you're happy."

Violet looked Sophia in the eyes, and took a deep breath to stop from cracking a smile.

"Sophia, I'm not happy to hear my girl say *fuck*."

As Sophia's breathing steadied and her eyes cooled off, she stomped back up the stairs to give her stuffed animals an update of the events and to rinse out her mouth. Violet continued making dinner and said under her breath to the overcooked pasta, "Or, if you hope that I am happy about how things are going so far, then — yes, Sophia, I am."